MW00344541

The route to y

When they look back at their formative years, many Indians nostalgically recall the vital part Amar Chitra Katha picture books have played in their lives. It was **ACK – Amar Chitra Katha** – that first gave them a glimpse of their glorious heritage.

Since they were introduced in 1967, there are now **over 400 Amar Chitra Katha** titles to choose from. **Over 90 million copies** have been sold worldwide.

Now the Amar Chitra Katha titles are even more widely available in **1000+ bookstores all across India**. Log on to www.ack-media.com to locate a bookstore near you. If you do not have access to a bookstore, you can buy all the titles through our online store **www.amarchitrakatha.com**. We provide quick delivery anywhere in the world.

To make it easy for you to locate the titles of your choice from our treasure trove of titles, the books are now arranged in five categories.

Epics and Mythology
Best known stories from the Epics and the Puranas

Indian Classics
Enchanting tales from Indian literature

Fables and Humour
Evergreen folktales, legends and tales of wisdom and humour

Bravehearts
Stirring tales of brave men and women of India

Visionaries
Inspiring tales of thinkers, social reformers and nation builders

Contemporary Classics
The Best of Modern Indian literature

Amar Chitra Katha Pvt Ltd
© Amar Chitra Katha Pvt Ltd, 2010, Reprinted April 2019,
ISBN 978-81-8482-383-7
Published by Amar Chitra Katha Pvt. Ltd., AFL House, 7th Floor,
Lok Bharati Complex,Marol Maroshi Road, Andheri (East), Mumbai - 400059, India.
Printed at Nitin Book Binding Works, Mumbai - 400015.
For Consumer Complaints Contact Tel : + 91-2249188881/2
Email: customerservice@ack-media.com

The route to your roots

THE LORD OF LANKA

Ambition and arrogance – these were to be the cause of Ravana's downfall. Blessed by both Brahma the creator and Shiva the destroyer, the powerful ruler of Lanka could have enjoyed fame and respect had he only reined in his arrogance. It was left to Vishnu the preserver to find a way to curb Ravana. In the process, there unfolded one of the world's most beautiful romantic sagas – the story of Rama's love for his devoted Sita.

Script
Anant Pai

Illustrations
Pulak Biswas

Editor
Anant Pai

THE LORD OF LANKA

SUMALI WAS THE KING OF THE RAKSHASAS. FROM THE NETHER-WORLD, WHERE HE LIVED, HE ONCE CAME TO VISIT THE WORLD OF MEN, ALONG WITH HIS BEAUTIFUL DAUGHTER, KAIKESI.

YOU SHALL MARRY THE WORTHIEST OF MEN AND BEAR MANY MIGHTY SONS.

HE TRAVELLED FROM ONE PLACE TO ANOTHER LOOKING FOR THE MAN. BUT—

KAIKESI, NOT ONE OF THEM IS GOOD ENOUGH.

AT LAST, ONE DAY, HE SAW A MAGNIFICENT CHARIOT DESCENDING FROM THE SKY IN FRONT OF THE HERMITAGE OF VISHRAVA, A GREAT SAGE.

THAT IS KUBERA, VISHRAVA'S SON. HOW NOBLE IS HIS BEARING! HE SEEMS RICH AND MIGHTY.

SUMALI RETURNED WITH HIS DAUGHTER TO THE NETHER-WORLD; BUT HE COULD NOT FORGET KUBERA.

DAUGHTER, APPROACH VISHRAVA. AND WIN HIM OVER. IF HE MARRIES YOU, YOU WILL HAVE SONS AS MIGHTY AS KUBERA.

ACCORDINGLY KAIKESI WENT TO THE HERMITAGE OF VISHRAVA. HE WAS BUSY OFFERING HIS EVENING PRAYERS.

O BEAUTIFUL MAIDEN! WHO ARE YOU? WHY HAVE YOU COME HERE?

MY NAME IS KAIKESI. YOU ARE A GREAT SAGE. YOU KNOW WHY.

I UNDERSTAND. BUT YOU HAVE COME TO ME AT THE WRONG HOUR. THE CHILDREN BORN TO US WILL BE WICKED RAKSHASAS...

LORD!

...THE YOUNGEST HOWEVER WILL BE A NOBLE ONE.

VISHRAVA MARRIED KAIKESI AND WITHIN A FEW YEARS, RAVANA, THE TEN-HEADED ONE, KUMBHAKARNA, SHOORPANAKHA, AND VIBHEE—SHANA WERE BORN.

YEARS ROLLED BY. RAVANA AND KUMBHAKARNA GREW UP TO BE ARROGANT AND AMBITIOUS. ONE DAY, KUBERA CAME TO VISIT HIS FATHER.

AFTER KUBERA HAD LEFT—

RAVANA, MY SON! LOOK AT KUBERA, THE KING OF LANKA. HE IS RICH AND POWERFUL. YOU MUST BE LIKE HIM.

MOTHER, HERE AND NOW I MAKE THIS VOW. I WILL EXCEL KUBERA.

RAVANA IMMEDIATELY SET OUT FOR GOKARNA ALONG WITH HIS BROTHERS, KUMBHAKARNA AND VIBHEESHANA. THEY BEGAN PERFORMING SEVERE PENANCES.

DURING THE PENANCE, RAVANA DID NOT TOUCH FOOD. ONE BY ONE HE SACRIFICED HIS HEADS IN THE HOLY FIRE.

WHEN HE WAS ABOUT TO SACRIFICE HIS TENTH HEAD, LORD BRAHMA APPEARED BEFORE HIM.

I AM PLEASED WITH YOU. ASK FOR A BOON.

O LORD, GRANT ME IMMORTALITY.

IMMORTALITY IS NOT FOR YOU. ASK FOR SOMETHING ELSE.

THEN LET ME NOT DIE AT THE HANDS OF GODS, DEMONS, RAKSHASAS SERPENTS AND SPIRITS. I AM NOT AFRAID OF MORTALS.

SO BE IT.

AND I GRANT YOU MORE. YOUR HEADS WILL BE RESTORED TO YOU. YOU WILL ALSO HAVE THE POWER TO CHANGE YOUR FORM AT WILL.

BRAHMA ALSO GRANTED BOONS TO VIBHEESHANA AND KUMBHAKARNA.

VIBHEESHANA, WHAT BOON DID LORD BRAHMA GRANT YOU?

IMMORTALITY. I HAD ONLY EXPRESSED THE WISH THAT I MIGHT NEVER SWERVE FROM THE PATH OF RIGHTEOUSNESS.

AND WHAT A FOOL I WAS! I ASKED FOR SLEEP FOR MANY YEARS.

WHEN THEY RETURNED HOME, SUMALI CAME TO MEET THEM.

RAVANA, I AM PROUD OF YOU. NOW WIN BACK LANKA. IT BELONGS RIGHTFULLY TO OUR PEOPLE.

PROMPTED BY THE WORDS OF SUMALI AND HIS MEN, RAVANA SET OUT FOR LANKA.

BROTHER! IT IS NOT PROPER.

QUIET, VIBHEESHANA. WHO ASKED FOR YOUR ADVICE?

FROM HIS CAMP IN THE JUNGLE OF THE TRIKOOTA MOUNTAINS, RAVANA SENT A MESSENGER TO THE COURT OF KUBERA.

GO AND TELL KUBERA THAT HE MUST VACATE LANKA, IMMEDIATELY. I WISH TO OCCUPY IT.

AT THE COURT OF KUBERA—

WHY DOES HE ASK ME TO VACATE LANKA? AFTER ALL, WHAT IS MINE IS HIS.

TELL RAVANA, I WILL CONSULT MY FATHER AND ACT.

KUBERA WENT TO VISHRAVA.

FATHER, TELL ME WHAT I SHOULD DO.

BRAHMA'S BOON HAS MADE RAVANA EVEN MORE ARROGANT. AGREE TO HIS WISH. GO TO MOUNT KAILAS. YOU WILL PROSPER THERE.

8

KUBERA VACATED LANKA. RAVANA CAME THERE WITH HIS ARMY AND BECAME THE KING.

AS THE DAYS PASSED, RAVANA BECAME INCREASINGLY ARROGANT. HE BEGAN HARASSING THE GODS, SAGES AND GANDHARVAS.

WHEN THE NEWS REACHED KUBERA—

RAVANA'S BEHAVIOUR IS BAD. IT IS MY DUTY TO CORRECT MY YOUNGER BROTHER.

HE SENT A MESSENGER TO LANKA.

MY MASTER, KUBERA SAYS, IT DOES NOT BEFIT THE RACE OF VISHRAVA TO HARASS SAGES AND KILL INNOCENT PEOPLE. YOU MUST MEND YOUR WAYS.

IMPUDENT MAN! YOU WILL PAY FOR THIS.

NOW I MUST TEACH KUBERA THE LESSON OF HIS LIFE.

MOUNTING HIS CHARIOT AND ACCOMPANIED BY A MIGHTY ARMY, RAVANA SPED TOWARDS KAILAS, KUBERA'S KINGDOM.

A GREAT BATTLE TOOK PLACE BETWEEN THE ARMIES OF RAVANA AND KUBERA.

BECAUSE OF THE BOON, RAVANA HAD RECEIVED FROM BRAHMA, NOTHING SEEMED TO HURT HIM...

...NOT EVEN THE MIGHTY MACE OF KUBERA.

AT LAST KUBERA FELL...

...BUT THE GODS WHO WERE WIT-NESSING THE BATTLE FROM ABOVE, TOOK HIM TO SAFETY IN A HEAVENLY CHARIOT.

THERE WAS NONE TO OBSTRUCT RAVANA NOW. HE SEIZED 'PUSHPAK', THE FLYING CHARIOT OF KUBERA, AND BEGAN EXPLORING MOUNT KAILAS.

SOON, HOWEVER, 'PUSHPAK' CAME TO A DEAD HALT.

WHEN RAVANA SAT BROODING ABOUT THE CAUSE...

...NANDI, SHIVA'S ATTENDANT, CAME DOWN.

RAVANA! THIS IS LORD SHIVA'S ABODE. DO NOT DISTURB HIM.

WHOSE ORDERS ARE THESE? SHIVA'S? I'LL UPROOT THIS VERY MOUNTAIN ON WHICH HE RESTS.

ASSUMING A HUGE FORM RAVANA TRIED TO LIFT KAILAS.

AS THE MOUNTAIN SHOOK, THE FOLLOWERS OF SHIVA WERE TERRIFIED.

O LORD! HELP! SAVE US!

EVEN PARVATI, LORD SHIVA'S CONSORT, WAS SCARED.

LORD!

DO NOT FEAR. I'M HERE.

LORD SHIVA PRESSED THE MOUNTAIN WITH HIS TOE AND RAVANA'S HANDS WERE CRUSHED BELOW IT.

AHH! HELP!

RAVANA'S MINISTER ADVISED HIM.

NONE OTHER THAN LORD SHIVA CAN SAVE YOU NOW. PROPITIATE HIM.

RAVANA BEGAN SINGING HYMNS IN PRAISE OF SHIVA.

PLEASED WITH HIM, LORD SHIVA PERMITTED RAVANA TO REMOVE HIS HANDS FROM UNDER THE MOUNTAIN...

...AND GAVE HIM A SWORD.

RAVANA! YOU ARE A MIGHTY WARRIOR.

RAVANA NOW ROAMED ABOUT THE WORLD, CONQUERING ALL WHOM HE MET.

ONE DAY, IN THE JUNGLES OF THE HIMALAYAS, HE SAW A BEAUTIFUL MAIDEN ENGAGED IN MEDITATION.

RAVANA ADVANCED TOWARDS HER.

O BEAUTIFUL MAIDEN, WHO ARE YOU? WHY DO YOU PERFORM SUCH AUSTERITIES?

I AM VEDAVATI. I AM PERFORMING THESE AUSTERITIES TO WIN LORD VISHNU AS MY HUSBAND.

I AM RAVANA, LORD OF LANKA. MARRY ME.

NONE OTHER THAN VISHNU CAN BE MY HUSBAND. GO AWAY.

RAVANA SEIZED HER BY HER HAIR.

ENRAGED, VEDAVATI CREATED A FIRE...

...AND JUMPED INTO IT.

I WILL BE BORN AGAIN AND BE THE CAUSE OF YOUR DEATH.

VEDAVATI TOOK BIRTH IN A LOTUS.

WHAT A BEAUTIFUL BABY! WHO COULD SHE BE?

RAVANA TOOK HER TO HIS CAMP. BUT—

SHE WILL BE THE CAUSE OF YOUR DEATH.

WHAT SHALL I DO WITH HER?

DISCARD HER.

RAVANA IMMEDIATELY THREW HER INTO THE RIVER.

MANY DAYS LATER, IN KING JANAKA'S *YAGNASHALA,* AT MITHILA—

BEFORE I BEGIN THIS FIRE SACRIFICE, I HAVE TO TILL THE SOIL SYMBOLICALLY.

SUDDENLY THERE APPEARED, IN THE CENTRE OF THE HALL, A BEAUTIFUL CHILD.

MY PRAYERS HAVE AT LAST BEEN ANSWERED. I'LL ADOPT HER AS MY CHILD.

IT WAS NONE OTHER THAN VEDAVATI.

SINCE I HAVE OBTAINED HER FROM A FURROW** I'LL NAME HER SITA.

SITA SOON GREW TO BE A BEAUTIFUL GIRL LOVED BY ONE AND ALL.

18

JANAKA ARRANGED A SWAYAMWARA TO WHICH HE INVITED PRINCES FROM FAR AND NEAR.

HE WHO SUCCEEDS IN STRINGING THIS BOW WILL WIN SITA'S HAND.

AMONG THE PRINCES WAS RAMA. OF AYODHYA, WHO HAD COME THERE WITH SAGE VISHWAMITRA.

RAMA LIFTED THE BOW EASILY. IT BROKE UNDER HIS STRENGTH.

HE MARRIED SITA AND CAME WITH HER TO AYODHYA WHERE THE PEOPLE WELCOMED THEM WARMLY.

MEANWHILE —

NOW I MUST CONQUER THE GODS IN HEAVEN.

SAVE US!

ONE NIGHT, WHEN RAVANA AND HIS MEN WERE RESTING ON MOUNT KAILAS, NEAR KUBERA'S CAPITAL ...

...HE SAW A BEAUTIFUL MAIDEN PASSING BY.

HE GOT UP FROM HIS SEAT AND STARTED MOVING TOWARDS HER.

WHO ARE YOU, FAIR MAIDEN?

LORD RAVANA! I AM RAMBHA.

GOOD. YOU KNOW MY NAME TOO.

I AM YOUR DAUGHTER-IN-LAW.

HOW CAN THAT BE?

RAMBHA TREMBLED.

I LOVE NALKOOBER, THE SON OF KUBERA, YOUR STEP-BROTHER. WE WILL SOON BE MARRIED.

RAVANA SEIZED HER BY HER ARM.

YOU SHALL MARRY ME.

BUT RAMBHA ESCAPED FROM HIS CLUTCHES. SHE WENT TO NALKOOBER AND NARRATED ALL.

RAVANA DARED TO THINK OF MARRYING YOU. IF HE EVER MARRIES A WOMAN AGAINST HER WILL, HIS HEADS WILL BREAK INTO SEVEN PIECES.

WHEN RAVANA HEARD THIS—

WHO IS AFRAID OF A WEAKLING'S CURSE?

BUT IN HIS HEART OF HEARTS HE TREMBLED.

YET, HE DID NOT STOP BEING WICKED.

ONE DAY, RAVANA CAME, DISGUISED AS A MONK, TO THE DANDAKA FOREST.

O BEAUTIFUL ONE, WHO ARE YOU? WHAT ARE YOU DOING HERE, ALONE IN THIS FOREST?

I AM SITA, WIFE OF RAMA, THE PRINCE OF AYODHYA. HE HAS GONE HUNTING...

...MY HUSBAND HAD TO COME TO LIVE IN THE FOREST TO FULFIL A PROMISE MADE BY HIS FATHER. WHO ARE YOU?

I AM RAVANA. I HAVE COME HERE TO TAKE YOU WITH ME. YOU WILL BE MY WIFE.

NEVER! GIVE UP SUCH THOUGHTS. YOU WILL ONLY INVITE DEATH BY COVETING ME.

UNDAUNTED RAVANA ASSUMED A HUGE FORM.

HE LIFTED HER...

...AND BROUGHT HER IN HIS CHARIOT TO LANKA.

AFTER HE HAD PLACED HER IN HIS ASHOKA GARDEN UNDER GUARD —

I LOVE YOU. WHY DO YOU WASTE YOUR TIME ON RAMA, WHO HAS BEEN BANISHED FROM HIS KINGDOM? MARRY ME.

RAVANA! YOUR DAYS ARE NUMBERED. MY LORD WILL SOON COME HERE AND KILL YOU.

ENRAGED, RAVANA ADVANCED TOWARDS HER...

...BUT FEAR KEPT HIM AWAY.

NO. NALKOOBER'S CURSE MAY COME TRUE. I MUST NOT MARRY A WOMAN AGAINST HER WILL.

MEANWHILE, RAMA WAS ON HIS WAY TO LANKA. HE HAD REACHED THE SHORE OF THE OCEAN WITH A HUGE ARMY OF MONKEYS AND BEARS.

RAVANA CALLED HIS BROTHERS AND COURTIERS.

WE MUST FIGHT AND KILL RAMA AND HIS ARMY.

BROTHER! IT IS ONLY PROPER THAT YOU RETURN SITA TO RAMA. HE WILL GO BACK IN PEACE.

RAVANA WAS ANGRY WITH VIBHEESHANA.

YOU CANNOT BEAR TO SEE MY MIGHT. YOU ARE A DISGRACE TO THE FAMILY. IF YOU WERE NOT MY BROTHER I WOULD HAVE KILLED YOU.

VIBHEESHANA, WITH FOUR OTHER RAKSHASAS FLEW INTO THE SKY...

...AND CAME TO THE CAMP OF RAMA.

RAMA! I SEEK YOUR PROTECTION.

YOU WILL BE SAFE HERE. I COUNT ON YOUR HELP.

SOON A BRIDGE WAS CONSTRUCTED ACROSS THE OCEAN AND...

...RAMA REACHED LANKA.

RAVANA BECAME IMPATIENT WITH SITA.

LISTEN, SITA! RAMA IS NO MORE. HE LIES DEAD IN THE BATTLEFIELD.

I DON'T BELIEVE YOU.

RAVANA TURNED TO ONE OF HIS WARRIORS.

GO AND FETCH THE HEAD OF RAMA.

WITHIN MINUTES, THE HEAD OF RAMA LAY IN FRONT OF SITA.

NOW, ARE YOU CONVINCED THAT RAMA IS DEAD? AND THIS IS HIS BOW. DON'T YOU RECOGNISE IT?

SITA, SHOCKED AT THE SIGHT, FELL UNCONSCIOUS.

WHEN SHE CAME BACK TO HER SENSES...

MY LORD! DEAD! WHAT SHALL I DO?

JUST THEN —

LORD! THE COMMANDER OF YOUR ARMY WANTS TO MEET YOU URGENTLY.

THE MOMENT RAVANA LEFT, RAMA'S HEAD AND BOW DISAPPEARED.

HOW DID THEY DISAPPEAR?

RAVANA DECEIVED YOU BY HIS MAGIC. DON'T GRIEVE, SITA. RAMA IS NOT DEAD.

RAMA WAS VERY MUCH ALIVE. LANKA WAS SOON CONVERTED INTO A BATTLEFIELD.

ONE BY ONE, THE WARRIORS OF RAVANA FELL.

THE MIGHTY KUMBHAKARNA PLAYED HAVOC ON THE MONKEY ARMY. BUT HE TOO FELL.

RAVANA HOWEVER CARRIED ON THE BATTLE.

WHEN HE FELL —

MY BROTHER! HOW I WISH YOU HAD HEEDED MY WORDS! YOUR PRIDE BROUGHT ABOUT THIS FALL.

DON'T GRIEVE, VIBHEESHANA! HE HAS DIED LIKE A BRAVE WARRIOR.

LANKA NOW HAD A NEW LORD — THE GOOD AND GENTLE VIBHEESHANA. RAMA HAD HIM CROWNED KING.

AFTER THE CROWNING OF VIBHEESHANA, RAMA RETURNED WITH SITA TO AYODHYA.

RAVANA HUMBLED

AN ARROGANT KING FINDS NEW FRIENDS

RAVANA HUMBLED

Ravana had soaring ambitions – he thought he could be the lord of the universe. But he was no match for the great destroyer Lord Shiva, or the mighty thousand-armed Kartaveerya Arjuna, or even the monkey king Vali of Kishkindha. These powerful lords were merely amused by Ravana's arrogance, and saw him off with friendly words and a respect he did not deserve.

Script
A.Saraswati

Illustrations
Ram Waeerkar

Editor
Anant Pai

AT THE FEET OF SHIVA

RAVANA HAD DRIVEN AWAY HIS STEP-BROTHER, KUBERA, AND HAD MADE HIMSELF LORD OF LANKA AND ALL ITS WEALTH...

...INCLUDING PUSHPAKA, KUBERA'S FABULOUS AERIAL CHARIOT, THAT MOVED AS ITS OWNER WILLED.

NO ONE DARE CHALLENGE ME NOW. I AM LORD OVER ALL.

RAVANA HAD REASON TO FEEL ALL-POWERFUL. FOR THE CHARIOT SOARED WITH EASE...

...OVER HILL AND DALE.

1

3

ATOP THE MOUNTAIN, AT THAT MOMENT, PARVATI, WHO HAD JUST HAD A TIFF WITH SHIVA, WAS WALKING AWAY IN A HUFF.

PARVATI...

COME BACK, PARVATI!

I WILL NEVER COME BACK.

PARVATI!

SUDDENLY, THE EARTH SHOOK...

...AND HUGE BOULDERS CAME TUMBLING DOWN.

PARVATI LOST HER BALANCE...

...AND ALMOST FELL.

SHE STEADIED HERSELF, HOWEVER...

...AND RAN...

...INTO THE ARMS OF SHIVA.

WH-WH- WHAT...WH- WH- WHO- WHO...

IT WAS RAVANA LIFTING THE MOUNTAIN, NONE ELSE.

SHIVA! IT'S HAPPENING AGAIN! THE MOUNTAIN...

SHIVA, PLEASE... PLEASE STOP THIS TERRIFYING TREMOR.

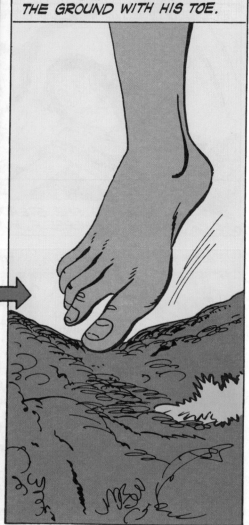

...AND SLOWLY PRESSED THE GROUND WITH HIS TOE.

SHIVA STOOD UP...

AND THE NEXT MOMENT...

...THE MOUNTAIN CAME DOWN ON RAVANA'S HANDS.

HE LET OUT A THUNDEROUS ROAR.

WHAT IS THAT?

AAAAAAHH!

IT IS THE CRY OF OUR FRIEND. THE ONE WHO CAUSED THE TREMOR THAT BROUGHT YOU BACK TO ME.

HE WAS LIFTING MOUNT KAILAS.

WHAT A COURAGEOUS BEING! FORGIVE HIM, MY LORD.

SOON—

THE BEING ON THIS MOUNTAIN IS MORE POWERFUL THAN I.

IF ONLY HE WOULD APPEAR BEFORE ME.

RAVANA, I SHIVA, AM PLEASED BY YOUR COURAGE AND PERSEVERANCE.

LORD SHIVA!

ARISE, RAVANA.

TO SHOW YOU HOW PLEASED I AM...

...I GIVE YOU CHANDRAHASA, MY INVINCIBLE SWORD.

RAVANA TOOK THE SWORD, BOWED TO SHIVA, ASCENDED HIS CHARIOT AND FLEW OFF.

THE MAHISHMATI EPISODE

ONCE AS RAVANA WAS ROAMING AROUND IN PUSHPAKA, WITH A FEW OF HIS MINISTERS, THEY CAME TO MAHISHMATI, THE KINGDOM OF KARTAVEERYA ARJUNA.

THE NARMADA! I WILL LAND ON THE BANK OF THIS HOLY RIVER.

WHAT A BEAUTIFUL SPOT!

SHALL BATHE IN THE RIVER AND WORSHIP SHIVA BEFORE WE MOVE ON.

SO—

KARTAVEERYA ARJUNA HAD CHOSEN THE SAME HOUR, BUT A SPOT MUCH FARTHER AWAY, TO SPORT IN THE RIVER WITH HIS WIVES.

MY LORD, WE AGREE THAT YOU ARE VERY STRONG. BUT CAN YOU CONTAIN NARMADA?

NO ONE CAN!

NOT EVEN YOU, THE THOUSAND-ARMED ARJUNA.

I'LL TAKE UP THE CHALLENGE!

11

ARJUNA SAT ON THE BED OF THE RIVER AND STRETCHED OUT HIS ARMS.

SOON, BEHIND ARJUNA THE BED OF THE RIVER RAN DRY...

...WHILE IN FRONT OF HIM THE WATER-LEVEL ROSE...

...AND THE RIVER OVERFLOWED ITS BANKS, SUBMERGING THE SURROUNDING LAND.

FURTHER UPSTREAM, MEANWHILE, RAVANA HAD COME OUT OF THE WATER, MADE A LINGA* OUT OF SAND...

...AND SAT DOWN TO PRAY WITH HIS MINISTERS KEEPING VIGIL.

WATCH THE RIVER. IT'S COMING CLOSER TO US!

IT IS IN FLOOD! AND THE MASTER IS MEDITATING!

WE DARE NOT DISTURB HIM! WHAT SHOULD WE DO?

21 Inspiring Stories of Courage

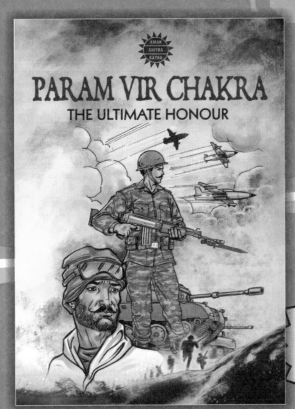

MRP
₹399/-

RAVANA THE MIGHTY

Script: Swarn Khandpur
Illustrated by: S.K. Parab

RAVANA, THE RAKSHASA KING OF LANKA, WAS A MIGHTY BEING. HIS STRENGTH WAS SO GREAT THAT HE COULD AGITATE THE SEAS AND SPLIT THE PEAKS OF MOUNTAINS.

ON THE BATTLEFIELD OF LANKA, RAMA WHO WAS SEEING HIM FOR THE FIRST TIME, EXCLAIMED, "AH! WHAT GLORY, WHAT EXCEEDING MAJESTY IS RAVANA'S! AS ONE CANNOT GAZE ON THE SUN, NEITHER CAN THE EYE REST ON HIM. SUCH IS THE BLINDING POWER OF HIS MAGNIFICENCE! NEITHER DEVAS, DANAVAS NOR HEROES POSSESS A BODY EQUAL TO HIS!"

RAMA AND RAVANA WERE SKILLED WARRIORS AND BOTH BROUGHT EXCEPTIONAL KNOWLEDGE IN THE SCIENCE OF ARMS TO THE FIGHT. WATCHING THE DREADFUL COMBAT BETWEEN THE TWO, THE DEVAS, THE GANDHARVAS, THE RISHIS, THE DANAVAS AND THE DAITYAS CRIED OUT, "AS THE SKY IS COMPARABLE ONLY WITH THE SKY AND THE OCEAN ONLY WITH THE OCEAN, SO IS THIS FIGHT BETWEEN RAMA AND RAVANA!"

RAMA'S VICTORY OVER RAVANA IS COMMEMORATED IN THE NORTH DURING THE FESTIVAL OF DUSSEHRA. FOR NINE DAYS RAMLILA IS ENACTED AND ON THE TENTH DAY, DUSSEHRA WHICH MARKS THE DAY OF VICTORY, AN EFFIGY OF RAVANA IS BURNT.

THE HUGE EFFIGY IS ERECTED ON A MIGHTY FRAMEWORK OF BAMBOOS. IT IS THEN FILLED WITH FIRE-CRACKERS AND COVERED ON THE OUTSIDE WITH COLOURED PAPERS.

ALTHOUGH RAVANA IS DESCRIBED IN THE RAMAYANA AS HAVING TEN HEADS, IN FOLK ART HE IS OFTEN SHOWN WITH ONLY NINE.

ON DUSSEHRA DAY, WHEN THE EFFIGY CATCHES FIRE, IT BLAZES IN FIERY SPLENDOUR TILL THE MIGHTY RAVANA FALLS.

THE MINISTERS WATCHED HELPLESSLY AS THE WATER GRADUALLY NEARED RAVANA.

AS IT BEGAN TO WASH AWAY THE LINGA, RAVANA'S PRAYERS ENDED AND HE OPENED HIS EYES.

THE RIVER SEEMS TO BE IN FLOOD, MASTER.

GO AND FIND OUT WHY.

SOON, THE MINISTER WAS BACK.

MASTER, A MIGHTY BEING HAS DAMMED THE RIVER WITH HIS MASSIVE TRUNK AND HIS ONE THOUSAND ARMS!

ONE THOUSAND ARMS! IT IS KARTAVEERYA ARJUNA!

HOW DARE HE!

HE SHALL MEET HIS END TODAY! LEAD ME TO HIM.

SO—

LOOK! MASTER! THERE HE IS!

AS ARJUNA STOOD UP NARMADA SLID BACK INTO HER BED AND RUSHED DOWNSTREAM.

ARJUNA STRODE OVER TO RAVANA.

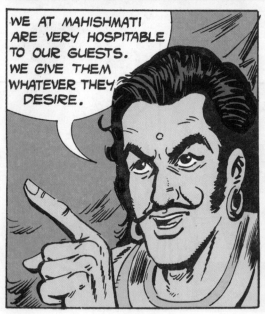

WE AT MAHISHMATI ARE VERY HOSPITABLE TO OUR GUESTS. WE GIVE THEM WHATEVER THEY DESIRE.

SO I WILL GIVE YOU THE BATTLE YOU CRAVE.

THE WEAPON THEY CHOSE WAS THE MACE. THE TWO MIGHTY KINGS FOUGHT LONG AND HARD.

AT LAST A BLOW FROM ARJUNA SENT RAVANA REELING...

THUD

...TO THE GROUND.

WHEN RAVANA'S GRANDFATHER, THE SAGE PULASTYA, LEARNT THAT ARJUNA HAD TAKEN HIS GRANDSON PRISONER, HE CAME TO MAHISHMATI.

WELCOME, REVERED ONE!

23

TELL ME HOW BEST I CAN SERVE YOU?

ARJUNA, YOU HAVE PROVED THAT NONE IS EQUAL TO YOU IN STRENGTH BY SUBDUING RAVANA.

NOW RELEASE MY GRANDSON.

AS YOU COMMAND, REVERED ONE.

ARJUNA SET RAVANA FREE, HONOURED HIM WITH GIFTS AND SEALED THEIR FRIENDSHIP WITH FIRE AS THE WITNESS.

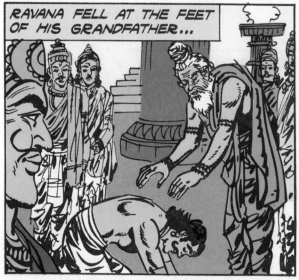

RAVANA FELL AT THE FEET OF HIS GRANDFATHER...

...AND LEFT MAHISHMATI WITH HIS MINISTERS.

TAILPIECE

ONE DAY RAVANA CAME TO THE CITY OF KISHKINDHA.

AH! THERE'S VALI, THE MONKEY KING. I WILL LAND HERE.

PUSHPAKA DUTIFULLY BROUGHT HIM DOWN AND RAVANA WALKED OUT.

SURELY, THE PUNY CREATURE SAW ME LAND. WHY DIDN'T HE GREET ME?

HE NEEDS TO BE HUMBLED FOR THIS.

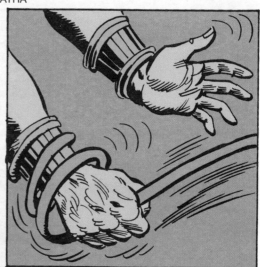

!!

SUDDENLY—

HEY!

VALI, THE MONKEY KING, HAD FINISHED HIS PRAYER ON THE EASTERN SHORE. HE WAS NOW OFF...

...TO THE WESTERN SHORE...

...FOR A HOLY DIP...

SPLASH

...AND MORE PRAYERS.

NOW IS THE TIME TO FREE MYSELF.

27

VALI TOOK OFF AGAIN.

AFTER PRAYING IN THE HIMALAYAS HE CAME DOWN TO THE SOUTHERN SHORE...

...FOR THE LAST DIP...

...AND THE LAST ROUND OF PRAYERS.

I MUST FREE MYSELF BEFORE HE LEAPS OFF AGAIN!

USING ALL HIS MIGHT, RAVANA KICKED OUT WITH HIS ONLY FREE LEG.

BUT—

NO!

VALI TOOK OFF AGAIN.

THIS TIME HE WAS ON HIS WAY HOME TO KISHKINDHA.

HELP! LET ME GO! LET ME GO!

SOMEBODY IS IN DISTRESS. BUT I DON'T SEE ANYONE.

WHERE ARE YOU?

HERE!

VALI SPUN ROUND —

WHERE?

HERE! HERE!

VALI SPUN ROUND AGAIN.

SOMEBODY IS TRYING TO MAKE A FOOL OF ME!

31

Mystique, Adventure and Magic

MRP ₹180/-

MAHIRAVANA

A MAGICIAN OUTWITTED

The route to your roots

MAHIRAVANA

When his rakshasa army was destroyed in the battle against Rama, the prince of Ayodhya, Ravana, the Lord of Lanka, called for his son Mahiravana, a powerful magician. Would he succeed in killing the noble Rama and Lakshmana? Not while Hanuman was around, for this faithful friend had a trick or two of his own. The Bengali "Krittivasa Ramayana" written by poet Krittivasa in the 15th century describes how Hanuman manages to get around the wily sorceror's schemes.

Script
Meera Ugra

Illustrations
Ram Waeerkar

Editor
Anant Pai

MAHIRAVANA

MAHIRAVANA, THE MAGICIAN KING OF THE NETHER WORLD, WAS RELAXING IN HIS PALACE ONE EVENING.

SUDDENLY, THROUGH HIS SUPER-NATURAL POWERS, HE PERCEIVED THAT SOMEONE WAS IN DANGER AND NEEDED HIS HELP.

BUT WHO? WHO IS THINKING OF ME? I MUST FIND OUT.

RETIRING TO HIS CHAMBER, HE TRIED TO FIGURE OUT WHO IT WAS.

NO ONE HERE IN THE NETHER WORLD NEEDS MY HELP.

NO ONE NEEDS ME IN HEAVEN, EITHER.

HE THEN THOUGHT OF HIS KITH AND KIN LIVING ON EARTH. THEN—

AH! IT'S MY FATHER! HE IS IN DANGER! I MUST GO TO HIM IMMEDIATELY.

AS HE CHANTED A MAGIC SPELL, THE ROOF OPENED TO GIVE HIM A PATH UPWARDS TOWARDS THE EARTH.

GLIDING OUT, MAHIRAVANA STARTED FOR LANKA, WHERE HIS FATHER, RAVANA, REIGNED.

I WONDER WHAT HAS HAPPENED! FATHER HAS MANY POWERFUL RELATIVES AND GENERALS TO HELP HIM. AND YET HE SUMMONS ME....

SOON HE ARRIVED AT LANKA.

IS IT TOO LATE? THE PLACE LOOKS DESERTED. WHAT COULD HAVE HAPPENED?

MEANWHILE, RAVANA WAITED IMPATIENTLY IN HIS PALACE FOR MAHIRAVANA.

WHY IS HE TAKING SO LONG?

JUST THEN—

FATHER!

YOU HAVE COME, MY SON! I KNEW YOU WOULD NOT FAIL ME.

I AM RELIEVED TO SEE YOU, FOR I AM IN TROUBLE.

I AM THREATENED BY AN ENEMY WHO HAS ALREADY KILLED KUMBHAKARNA, INDRAJIT AND MANY OTHER MIGHTY WARRIORS.

KUMBHAKARNA AND INDRAJIT! HOW DID IT HAPPEN, FATHER? WHO IS THIS ENEMY WHO IS SO POWERFUL?

LISTEN, SON, AND I WILL TELL YOU THE WHOLE STORY.

MY SISTER WAS INSULTED BY PRINCE RAMA. TO AVENGE THE INSULT, I KIDNAPPED HIS WIFE, SITA.

THEN RAMA SENT HANUMAN, A MONKEY, IN SEARCH OF SITA. HE CAME TO LANKA AND DESTROYED MY PRECIOUS ASHOKA GROVE.

I MANAGED TO HAVE HIM BOUND AND ORDERED HIS TAIL TO BE SET ON FIRE.

THE WRETCHED MONKEY JUMPED FROM ROOF TO ROOF AND VERY SOON MY CITY WAS ABLAZE.

THEN RAMA CAME WITH HIS MONKEY ARMY.

HE KILLED MANY OF MY BRAVE GENERALS AND WARRIORS.

AND THAT IS WHY I NOW NEED YOUR HELP.

I CAN'T BELIEVE IT! YOU, WHO HAVE DEFEATED INDRA AND OTHER DEVAS, HAVE BEEN DEFEATED BY A BANISHED PRINCE AND A MONKEY-KING!

THEY ARE NOT ORDINARY HUMAN BEINGS, SON! THEIR VALOUR IS GREATER THAN THAT OF EVEN THE DEVAS.

OH, IF ONLY YOU HAD CALLED ME EARLIER! ALL OUR KINSMEN AND FRIENDS WOULD HAVE BEEN SAVED!

BUT, EVEN NOW, YOU CAN HELP US TO VANQUISH THE ENEMY, SON.

AND THEY STARTED MAKING PLANS.

MEANWHILE, IN RAMA'S CAMP, VIBHEESHANA* WAS ANXIOUS TO KNOW WHAT RAVANA'S NEXT MOVE WOULD BE.

OF COURSE, VIBHEESHANA, IF YOU THINK IT IS NECESSARY.

MY LORD, ALL RAVANA'S MEN HAVE BEEN KILLED IN BATTLE. MAY I GO AND FIND OUT WHAT HE PLANS TO DO NEXT?

*RAVANA'S BROTHER WHO HAD JOINED THE OPPOSITE CAMP

VIBHEESHANA ASSUMED THE FORM OF A BIRD AND FLEW OFF...

...TILL HE CAME TO RAVANA'S PALACE.

SO, THIS IS IT—RAVANA HAS SUMMONED MAHIRAVANA!

HE HURRIED BACK—

RAMA MUST BE INFORMED OF THIS!

REGAINING HIS NORMAL FORM, HE WENT TO RAMA.

O RAMA! RAVANA HAS SUMMONED MAHIRAVANA, WHO IS BRAVE AND SKILFUL BUT...

BUT WHAT? GO ON, VIBHEESHANA.

... IT'S HIS MAGICAL POWERS WHICH ARE TO BE FEARED MOST. HE IS A WILY PERSON. ONE CANNOT FORETELL HIS PLANS.

I SEE....

WE MUST BE VERY CAREFUL. TONIGHT SPECIALLY WE MUST BE ALERT AND VIGILANT.

WE WILL KEEP AWAKE AND FOIL MAHIRAVANA IF HE TRIES TO PLAY ANY OF HIS TRICKS.

BUT WE MUST ALSO THINK OF A WAY OF KEEPING RAMA AND LAKSHMANA SAFE TONIGHT.

HANUMAN WAS DEEP IN THOUGHT. THEN—

YES! I HAVE IT! I'LL BUILD A STRONG FORT- RESS AROUND RAMA AND LAKSHMANA SO THAT NO ONE WILL BE ABLE TO GET IN.

A FORTRESS? IN SUCH A SHORT TIME?

YES. YOU JUST WATCH!

BUT BEFORE I BEGIN, LORD RAMA, I HAVE A REQUEST TO MAKE. SET THE POWERFUL DISCUS, SUDARSHAN, ON GUARD AT THE TOP OF THE FORTRESS.

AS YOU WISH HANUMAN.

AND THEN, HANUMAN STARTED EXTENDING HIS TAIL. IT STOOD STIFF AND WENT HIGHER AND HIGHER...

...TILL IT REACHED THE SKY. IT BECAME A HUNDRED YOJANAS* LONG. THEN HE TURNED TO SUGREEVA, THE KING OF THE MONKEYS.

O KING, PLEASE SIT THERE AND HOLD RAMA ON YOUR LAP.

ANGADA WILL LIKEWISE PROTECT YOU, LAKSHMANA.

RAMA SAT ON SUGREEVA'S LAP AND LAKSHMANA SAT ON ANGADA'S LAP.

NOW OUR ENTIRE ARMY WILL POSITION ITSELF IN A CIRCLE AROUND THEM.

WE'LL DO THAT.

*ONE YOJANA = 13 KILOMETRES

THEN HANUMAN STARTED MAKING THE FORTRESS.

IT WAS COMPLETED SOON. THE DISCUS, SUDARSHAN, GUARDED THE SUMMIT.

VIBHEESHANA, YOU WILL KEEP GUARD ALL AROUND THE FORTRESS AND I'LL WATCH THE ENTRANCE. WE ARE NOW FULLY PREPARED FOR MAHIRAVANA.

YOU ARE RIGHT, HANUMAN. STILL...

...WE MUST BE VERY, VERY CAREFUL. THAT MAGICIAN CAN ASSUME ANY GUISE. SO PLEASE DON'T LET ANYONE ENTER THE FORTRESS — NOT EVEN YOUR OWN FATHER, PAWAN.*

DON'T WORRY, VIBHEESHANA, I WON'T. NO ONE WILL BE ALLOWED TO GET IN.

WHEN NIGHT FELL, THEY CONTINUED THEIR VIGIL.

*THE WIND GOD

MEANWHILE, IN LANKA, RAVANA AND MAHIRAVANA WERE NOT IDLE. THEY, TOO, WERE MAKING CAREFUL PLANS.

NOW FATHER, LEAVE EVERYTHING TO ME. I'LL TAKE RAMA AND LAKSHMANA AWAY TO THE NETHER WORLD AND SACRIFICE THEM THERE TO THE GODDESS, DURGA.

YOU HAVE TAKEN A LOAD OFF MY CHEST, SON.

MAHIRAVANA DEPARTED. HE TOOK NO MEN, NO HORSES AND NO WEAPONS. ENDOWED AS HE WAS WITH MAGIC POWERS, WITHIN MINUTES HE HAD REACHED RAMA'S CAMP.

HMM...VERY CLEVER! THE DISCUS BARS THE WAY FROM THE SKY.

RAMA AND LAKSHMANA MUST BE IN THAT FORTRESS. BUT HOW SHALL I GET PAST THE MONKEY TO REACH THEM?

THAT WAS INDEED A DIFFICULT PROBLEM, FOR HANUMAN WAS KEEPING A STRICT WATCH.

I WILL KEEP GUARD ROUND THE FORTRESS. REMEMBER, NOT EVEN YOUR FATHER IS TO BE ALLOWED IN.

BUT SOON AFTER VIBHEESHANA LEFT—

O MIGHTY HANUMAN! I AM DASHARATHA, RAMA'S FATHER. LET ME ENTER. I WANT TO MEET MY SONS.

KING DASHARATHA!

PLEASE WAIT FOR A MINUTE, MY LORD. VIBHEESHANA WILL SOON BE COMING THIS WAY AND WILL TAKE YOU IN.

AH! HERE HE COMES.

KING DASHARATHA IS HERE, VIBHEESHANA, TO MEET HIS SONS.

KING DASHARATHA? I SEE NO ONE HERE!

HERE.... OH! BUT WHERE HAS HE GONE?

IT MUST HAVE BEEN MAHIRAVANA IN DISGUISE! BE CAREFUL NOW. REMEMBER, YOU ARE NOT TO LET ANYONE ENTER.

HE WON'T FOOL ME AGAIN, O NOBLE ONE!

AS SOON AS VIBHEESHANA LEFT ON HIS ROUNDS—

O HANUMAN, I HAVE NOT SEEN MY BROTHERS FOR A VERY LONG TIME! PLEASE LET ME GO IN.

PRINCE BHARATA! YOUR BROTHERS WILL BE HAPPY TO MEET YOU. BUT PLEASE WAIT FOR VIBHEESHANA.

BUT WHEN VIBHEESHANA CAME THERE—

HERE COMES VIBHEESHANA. HE'LL ESCORT YOU ....

TO WHOM ARE YOU TALKING? THERE'S NO ONE HERE!

I WAS TALKING TO PRINCE BHARATA. BUT...WHERE HAS HE GONE?

MAHIRAVANA IS UP TO HIS TRICKS AGAIN, HANUMAN. YOU MUST REMEMBER MY WARNING—NOT EVEN YOUR FATHER IS TO ENTER!

VIBHEESHANA LEFT ON HIS ROUNDS AGAIN.

SOON AFTER—

YOU ARE BACK VERY QUICKLY, VIBHEESHANA! YOU JUST PASSED THIS WAY A FEW SECONDS AGO.

I DIDN'T COMPLETE MY ROUND, HANUMAN. FEAR OF THE CUNNING MAHIRAVANA BROUGHT ME BACK.

I AM GOING IN TO TIE THESE PROTECTIVE STRINGS ROUND THE WRISTS OF RAMA AND LAKSHMANA.

ALL RIGHT, VIBHEESHANA.

THE NEXT MOMENT—

VIBHEESHANA, WHEN DID YOU COME OUT? I DIDN'T SEE YOU COMING OUT.

COMING OUT FROM WHERE, MY FRIEND? I HAVE BEEN OUT ALL THE TIME.

B...BUT...YOU WENT IN JUST NOW—TO TIE PROTECTIVE STRINGS ON THE WRISTS OF RAMA AND LAKSHMANA. OR, ARE YOU....

WHAT ARE YOU TALKING ABOUT? I DIDN'T GO IN AT ALL!

YOU ARE LYING! YOU ARE A SPY OF RAVANA, I AM SURE! YOU PLAYED THIS TRICK UPON US... YOU...!

CALM DOWN, HANUMAN. IT SEEMS THE CLEVER MAHIRAVANA HAS TRICKED YOU BY COMING IN MY GUISE THIS TIME.

YOU COULD BE RIGHT! LET'S GO IN AND SEE.

FEAR GRIPPED THEM BOTH. THEY RUSHED INSIDE.

16

LOOK!

RAMA AND LAKSHMANA ARE NOT HERE!

EVERY ONE IS FAST ASLEEP. AS IF BY MAGIC....

THIS IS MAHIRAVANA'S WORK! SPRINKLING THIS MAGIC POWDER BEFORE THEM...

...HE PUT THE MIGHTY WARRIORS TO SLEEP AND CARRIED RAMA AND LAKSHMANA AWAY WITH HIM THROUGH THE TUNNEL.

ALL IS LOST! PLEASE FORGIVE ME, VIBHEESHANA, FOR SUSPECTING YOU.

DON'T WORRY ABOUT THAT, HANUMAN. LET'S WAKE THE OTHERS UP.

WAKE UP, O SUGREEVA! WAKE UP, ANGADA!

SOON, EVERYONE WAS WIDE AWAKE.

O KING SUGREEVA! RAMA AND LAKSHMANA HAVE BEEN CARRIED AWAY BY MAHIRAVANA. I AM NOT FIT TO LIVE! IT WAS ALL MY FAULT.

NO! AS YOUR KING, THE BLAME MUST FALL ON ME.

—AND ON ME TOO. I HAVE FAILED IN MY DUTY!

THEN JAMBAVAN, THE WISE ONE, SPOKE OUT.

THE BLAME MUST BE SHARED EQUALLY BY ALL OF US. BUT WHY WASTE TIME? LET US THINK OF A WAY OF RESCUING THEM. HANUMAN SHOULD GO AND FIND THEM.

YES. IF ANYONE CAN FIND THEM, IT IS HANUMAN.

O HANUMAN, YOU CROSSED THE MIGHTY OCEAN TO RESCUE SITA. ONLY YOU CAN PERFORM THIS TASK NOW. WE DEPEND UPON YOU.

MY HEAD BOWS LOW WITH SHAME, MY LORD, FOR I LET THE DEAR ONES BE CARRIED AWAY UNDER OUR VERY EYES!

TO ATONE I'LL SEARCH THE THREE WORLDS TILL I FIND THEM, FOR WITHOUT THEM I CANNOT LIVE.

HANUMAN'S TAIL CAME BACK TO ITS NORMAL SIZE. BIDDING THEM FAREWELL, HANUMAN ENTERED THE TUNNEL MADE BY MAHIRAVANA.

HE TRAVELLED THROUGH THE LONG TUNNEL...

...TILL AT LAST HE REACHED THE END.

THE NETHER WORLD STRETCHED OUT IN FRONT OF HIM.

HOW SHALL I FIND THEM IN THIS VAST PLACE?

HE SEARCHED ONE TOWN AFTER ANOTHER IN THE NETHER WORLD. AT LAST—

AH! THIS LOOKS LIKE MAHIRAVANA'S CAPITAL! I FEEL CERTAIN I'LL FIND RAMA AND LAKSHMANA HERE.

THEN HE SAW A BEAUTIFUL LAKE. ASSUMING A VERY SMALL FORM, HE WAITED ON A HIGH TREE.

I HOPE NO ONE WILL NOTICE ME.

BUT HE WAS SPOTTED BY SOME WOMEN WHO HAD COME THERE TO FETCH WATER.

LOOK! A MONKEY!

HOW TINY IT IS!

I WONDER WHERE IT HAS COME FROM!

A MONKEY HERE? THIS DOES NOT AUGUR WELL FOR OUR KING.

WHY? OUR KING FEARS NOTHING. HE IS STRONGER THAN ANYONE IN THE THREE WORLDS!

YES, BUT HE IS NOT IMMORTAL. ACCORDING TO A PROPHECY HE WILL MEET HIS END WHEN MONKEYS AND MEN COME HERE—AND HERE IS A MONKEY.

AND I HEAR THAT OUR KING HAS BROUGHT TWO MEN HERE AS HIS CAPTIVES!

TWO MEN! THEN MY LORD RAMA AND HIS BROTHER ARE HERE!

I MUST NOT WASTE ANY TIME.

JUST THEN A TERRIBLE DIN STARTLED HIM.

WHAT IS THAT NOISE? WHAT'S HAPPENING AT THE PALACE?

TELL US, OLD MOTHER, WHY ARE SO MANY PRIESTS HURRYING TOWARDS THE PALACE?

IT'S A SECRET. I CAN'T TELL YOU ABOUT IT.

NO, NO. YOU MUST TELL US!

YES, YOU MUST!

ALL RIGHT. COME CLOSER.

BUT YOU MUST NOT TELL ANYONE ELSE, OR I'LL BE IN TROUBLE!

WE WON'T TELL A SINGLE PERSON.

HANUMAN BECAME VERY ATTENTIVE.

IN A SHORT WHILE, TWO HUMAN BEINGS WILL BE SACRIFICED TO THE GODDESS DURGA.

WHO ARE THEY?

WHERE HAVE THEY COME FROM?

WHERE ARE THEY NOW?

THEY ARE THE MOST HANDSOME CREATURES I HAVE EVER SEEN! POOR SOULS! AT THE MOMENT THEY ARE LOCKED UP IN A SECRET ROOM. BUT...ENOUGH... NO MORE. OFF YOU GO... AND REMEMBER YOUR PROMISE.

WE'LL BE ABSOLUTELY SILENT, MOTHER.

HANUMAN JUMPED DOWN FROM THE TREE...

I MUST HURRY NOW.

22

...AND FOLLOWING IN THE DIRECTION OF THE NOISE, HE QUICKLY FOUND MAHIRAVANA'S PALACE.

HE SEARCHED EVERYWHERE TILL HE CAME TO A TEMPLE.

AH — THIS SEEMS TO BE THE PLACE WHERE THE SACRIFICE IS TO BE PERFORMED.

INSIDE THE TEMPLE HE FOUND A SECRET CHAMBER—

THEY ARE HERE! AT LAST I HAVE FOUND THEM!

ASSUMING THE FORM OF A FLY...

...HANUMAN FLEW INTO THE CHAMBER.

23

THEN HE REGAINED HIS NORMAL FORM.

WAKE UP, MY LORDS! I HAVE COME TO RESCUE YOU!

RAMA AND LAKSHMANA GOT UP WITH A START.

WHERE ARE WE?

WHAT'S HAPPENING?

YOU ARE IN THE NETHER WORLD, THE PRISONERS OF MAHIRAVANA. HE BROUGHT YOU HERE USING HIS MAGICAL POWERS.

HOW CAN WE FIGHT THESE RAKSHASAS? I DON'T EVEN HAVE MY WEAPONS WITH ME.

I'LL FIGHT THE RAKSHASAS, O RAMA. LET ME, YOUR EVER FAITHFUL SERVANT, DESTROY THIS MAGICIAN ONCE AND FOR ALL.

HANUMAN THEN TOLD THEM OF MAHIRA-VANA'S PLANS TO SACRIFICE THEM TO DURGA.

LISTEN, O RAMA. ON MY WAY HERE, I SAW GODDESS DURGA. I'LL GO AND ASK HER FOR HELP.

ALL I NEED NOW IS YOUR BLESSING, MY LORD!

YOU ARE A TRUE FRIEND, HANUMAN. MAY YOU BE SUCCESSFUL.

ONCE AGAIN ASSUMING THE FORM OF A FLY, HANUMAN FLEW TO THE GODDESS.

SALUTATIONS, O GODDESS! I AM HANUMAN, A SERVANT OF RAMA.

THE EVIL MAHIRAVANA INTENDS TO SACRIFICE RAMA AND LAKSHMANA TO YOU. TELL ME, HAS THIS BEEN ORDERED BY YOU?

NO, NO! I HAVE NOT ORDERED ANY SACRIFICE!

BUT MAHIRAVANA WORSHIPS YOU. WILL YOU HELP HIM? FOR IF YOU DO....

DON'T BE IMPATIENT, HANUMAN. LISTEN TO ME FIRST.

MAHIRAVANA WANTS TO GET RID OF HIS ENEMIES. THAT IS WHY HE IS SACRIFICING THEM. HE IS NOT DOING IT TO PLEASE ME.

SO YOU WON'T HELP HIM?

NO! I WON'T HELP HIM! MAHIRAVANA HAS STARTED PERSECUTING THE NOBLE AND THE INNOCENT. HIS END IS NEAR.

GOOD! THEN TELL ME HOW TO DESTROY HIM.

LISTEN CAREFULLY. RAMA AND LAKSHMANA WILL BE BROUGHT HERE SOON. YOU SHOULD ACCOMPANY THEM UNSEEN AND THEN....

WHEN THE GODDESS HAD FINISHED TELLING HANUMAN THE COURSE TO TAKE—

THANK YOU, O GODDESS! YOU HAVE SOLVED ALL MY PROBLEMS.

HANUMAN THEN RETURNED TO RAMA AND ASSUMED HIS OWN FORM.

THE GODDESS WAS VERY HELPFUL, MY LORD. SHE HAS SUGGESTED A CLEVER PLAN.

GOOD. TELL ME THE PLAN QUICKLY FOR THERE IS VERY LITTLE TIME LEFT.

HANUMAN TOLD RAMA WHAT WAS TO BE DONE.

SOON—

BRING THE PRISONERS OUT.

HANUMAN MADE HIMSELF INVISIBLE AND FOLLOWED RAMA AND LAKSHMANA TO THE TEMPLE.

HA...HA! IT'S THE MIGHTY RAMA! YOU WERE VERY AMBITIOUS INDEED, RAMA, TO HAVE CHALLENGED MY FATHER! TODAY YOUR LIFE IS IN MY HANDS.

SOON YOU'LL DIE AND MY FATHER WILL MARRY SITA.

THE RITUAL BEGAN—

ALMIGHTY GODDESS! I BOW TO YOU!

HAND ME THE SWORD.

AFTER PURIFYING THE SWORD, HE OFFERED IT TO THE GODDESS.

ACCEPT THIS OFFERING, O GODDESS!

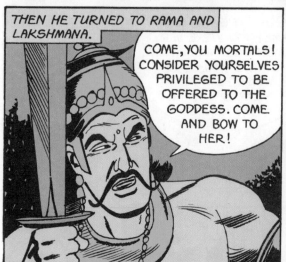

THEN HE TURNED TO RAMA AND LAKSHMANA.

COME, YOU MORTALS! CONSIDER YOURSELVES PRIVILEGED TO BE OFFERED TO THE GODDESS. COME AND BOW TO HER!

BUT THEY DIDN'T BUDGE.

MAHIRAVANA WAS ENRAGED.

WHAT? DIDN'T YOU HEAR ME? YOU DARE TO DISOBEY ME! COME FORWARD AND BOW!

WE ARE PRINCES OF AYODHYA, MAHIRAVANA. PEOPLE BOW TO US! WE HAVE NEVER BOWED TO ANY ONE IN OUR LIFE.

WE DON'T KNOW HOW TO BOW. YOU MUST SHOW US FIRST. THEN WE'LL DO IT.

YOU ARROGANT FOOLS! DON'T YOU KNOW HOW TO BOW?

ALL RIGHT! I'LL SHOW YOU!

HE BOWED LOW BEFORE THE SACRIFICIAL ALTAR.

SEIZING THIS OPPORTUNITY, HANUMAN ASSUMED HIS NORMAL FORM AND SPRANG FORWARD.

HE GRABBED THE SWORD AND...

...STRUCK! THE LORD OF THE NETHER WORLD LAY DEAD!

WITH TWO MORE BLOWS, HANUMAN SMASHED THE CHAINS THAT BOUND RAMA AND LAKSHMANA.

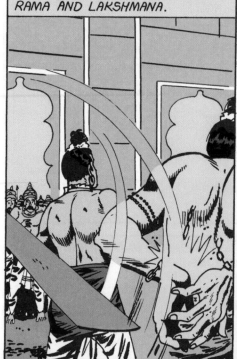

THEN HE TURNED TO DEAL WITH THE DEMONS—

COME FORWARD IF YOU WISH TO CHALLENGE ME. DO YOU DARE?

RUN!

WITHOUT MAHIRAVANA WE ARE LOST!

YOU ACTED PROMPTLY, BRAVE HANUMAN! YOU SAVED OUR LIVES TODAY.

I AM YOUR HUMBLE SERVANT AS ALWAYS, MY LORD.

SOON THEY STARTED ON THEIR JOURNEY BACK.

MEANWHILE IN SUGREEVA'S CAMP—

IT IS PAST NOON AND THEY HAVE NOT YET RETURNED. WHAT COULD HAVE HAPPENED TO THEM?

I'M SURE HANUMAN WILL NOT FAIL. LET'S TRY TO REMAIN CALM.

JUST THEN—

LOOK, KING SUGREEVA! THEY'VE COME!

MAHIRAVANA IS DEAD, FRIENDS.

AND RAVANA HAS NO ONE LEFT TO FIGHT FOR HIM!

HE'LL HAVE TO COME TO THE BATTLEFIELD HIMSELF TO FIGHT. AND THEN...

...VICTORY WILL BE OURS!

VICTORY TO RAMA!

KUMBHAKARNA

THE SLEEPING GIANT

The route to your roots

KUMBAKARNA

The only way Kumbhakarna could be kept out of mischief was to make him sleep twenty-four hours a day! Nothing would rouse this hulking ogre – not the trumpeting and trampling of elephants, not the deafening din of drums, and certainly not a rain of rocks. But when the aroma of fresh cooking wafted across his nose, he was up in a trice! However, that mightiest of warriors – Rama of Ayodhya – was lying in wait.

Script
Subba Rao & Nandini Das

Illustrations
Ram Waeerkar

Editor
Anant Pai

Cover illustration by: C.M. Vitankar

KUMBHAKARNA

KUMBHAKARNA WAS THE YOUNGER BROTHER OF RAVANA, THE TEN-HEADED RAKSHASA KING OF LANKA. HE WAS STRONG, BUT SAD TO SAY, HE WAS A BIG BULLY. HE LOVED TO FRIGHTEN AND HURT THOSE WHO WERE WEAKER THAN HIM.

RAVANA, DO YOU KNOW WHAT I'VE DONE TODAY? I WALKED INTO THE DANDAKA FOREST AND FRIGHTENED THE SAGES THERE! HA! HA! HA! YOU SHOULD HAVE SEEN THEM RUN!

WELL DONE, KUMBHAKARNA! I AM PLEASED.

BUT WHAT KUMBHAKARNA HAD DONE MADE HIS YOUNGER BROTHER VIBHISHANA UNHAPPY.

KUMBHAKARNA, WHAT HARM HAVE THOSE SAGES DONE YOU? WHY DON'T YOU LEAVE THEM ALONE?

1

DON'T LISTEN TO HIM, KUMBHAKARNA. YOU CARRY ON WITH YOUR WORK.

IF YOU DO, WE'LL HAVE TO FACE INDRA'S ANGER.

INDRA, KING OF THE DEVAS, WAS INDEED ANGRY.

I WON'T LET KUMBHAKARNA HARASS THE SAGES. I'LL TEACH HIM TO BEHAVE!

AND INDRA WITH HIS ARMY OF DEVAS ATTACKED KUMBHAKARNA.

KUMBHAKARNA, I'VE COME TO PUNISH YOU FOR BEING SO CRUEL.

COME, INDRA. I WAS WAITING FOR YOU.

INDRA HURLED HIS MACE AT KUMBHAKARNA.

BUT—

OH! NO! HE HAS SWALLOWED IT!

THEN KUMBHAKARNA LEAPT FORWARD...

...CAUGHT HOLD OF INDRA'S ELEPHANT BY ITS TUSKS...

...AND FLUNG IT FAR AWAY.

INDRA'S ARMY FLED IN TERROR.

WHEN KUMBHAKARNA TOLD RAVANA WHAT HE HAD DONE—

NO ONE CAN BEAT YOU, KUMBHAKARNA. YOU'RE THE MIGHTIEST OF THE MIGHTY.

THEN WHY DON'T WE CONQUER THE THREE WORLDS?

NOT YET. WE'RE STRONG AND POWERFUL. BUT WE MUST PRAY TO LORD BRAHMA AND GET MORE STRENGTH AND MORE POWER.

THEN LET'S DO SO.

WHAT ABOUT YOU, VIBHISHANA?

I TOO WANT TO PRAY TO LORD BRAHMA, BUT FOR A DIFFERENT REASON.

THE THREE BROTHERS WENT TO A LONELY, QUIET PLACE AND BEGAN TO PLEASE BRAHMA BY THINKING ONLY OF HIM AND NOTHING ELSE.

BRAHMA WAS PLEASED. HE APPEARED BEFORE THEM.

RAVANA, YOU WILL BE THE LORD OF THE THREE WORLDS.

WHEN INDRA HEARD THAT, HE WAS WORRIED.

BEFORE BRAHMA GIVES KUMBHAKARNA A BOON, I MUST DO SOMETHING.

HE WENT TO SARASWATI, THE GODDESS OF SPEECH.

O SARASWATI, ONLY YOU CAN SAVE US NOW.

HOW CAN I HELP YOU?

WHEN KUMBHAKARNA ASKS FOR A BOON, WILL YOU CAST A SPELL ON HIS TONGUE?

LEAVE IT TO ME. I'LL MAKE HIM ASK FOR A FOOLISH BOON.

MEANWHILE VIBHISHANA TOO HAD BEEN GIVEN A BOON. NOW IT WAS KUMBHAKARNA'S TURN.

WHAT DO YOU WANT, KUMBHAKARNA?

BEFORE KUMBHAKARNA COULD SPEAK, SARASWATI CAST HER SPELL!

I WANT TO SLEEP ALL THE TIME, MY LORD!

MAY YOU SLEEP FOR TWENTY-FOUR HOURS A DAY!

KUMBHAKARNA!

MY LORD, MY BROTHER DIDN'T KNOW WHAT HE WAS ASKING FOR. PLEASE TAKE BACK THE BOON.

I CANNOT TAKE BACK A BOON I HAVE GRANTED.

BUT IF KUMBHAKARNA SLEEPS ALL THE TIME AND NEVER WAKES UP, HIS ENEMIES WILL KILL HIM!

HAVE MERCY ON HIM, MY LORD.

ALL RIGHT. HE WILL REMAIN AWAKE FOR A WHOLE DAY, ONCE EVERY SIX MONTHS. BUT...

...IF ANYONE WAKES HIM UP ON ANY OTHER DAY, HIS LIFE WILL BE IN DANGER.

THE NEXT MOMENT—

HE'S FAST ASLEEP. WE'LL HAVE TO CARRY HIM HOME.

THERE GOES KUMBHAKARNA! WE'RE SAFE!

RAVANA AND VIBHISHANA TOOK KUMBHAKARNA TO HIS PALACE AND GENTLY LAID HIM ON HIS BED.

RAVANA, AREN'T YOU SAD ABOUT KUMBHAKARNA?

NOT REALLY. ON THE DAYS HE WAKES UP, HE WILL DO WHAT OTHERS COULDN'T IN A HUNDRED YEARS.

BRAHMA'S BOON TO RAVANA ALSO CAME TRUE. HE SOON BECAME THE MASTER OF THE THREE WORLDS.

EVEN THE SUN CAN'T SHINE WITHOUT MY PERMISSION.

DON'T BOAST, RAVANA. USE YOUR STRENGTH FOR THE GOOD OF OTHERS. A GOOD KING SHOULD BE KIND, HUMBLE AND JUST.

INSTEAD OF TAKING HIS BROTHER'S ADVICE, RAVANA CARRIED AWAY SITA, THE WIFE OF RAMA, THE PRINCE OF AYODHYA.

O RAMA... SAVE ME... RAMA...

AT LANKA, RAVANA KEPT SITA IN HIS ASHOKA GARDEN WHICH WAS FAR AWAY FROM HIS PALACE. VIBHISHANA CAME TO SEE HIM.

WHAT YOU'VE DONE IS WRONG. SITA IS RAMA'S WIFE. TAKE HER BACK TO HIM.

DON'T YOU DARE TELL ME WHAT I SHOULD DO!

IF YOU DON'T TAKE SITA BACK TO RAMA, I'LL GO AWAY FROM LANKA.

AND I WON'T STOP YOU!

VIBHISHANA LEFT AND WENT TO RAMA WHO WAS MARCHING TOWARDS LANKA WITH A HUGE ARMY OF MONKEYS.

RAMA, YOU ARE GOOD. I'M ON YOUR SIDE. I'VE COME TO SERVE YOU, TO FIGHT FOR YOU.

WELCOME, VIBHISHANA.

WITH THE HELP OF THE MONKEYS, RAMA BUILT A BRIDGE ACROSS THE SEA TO LANKA. HIS BROTHER LAKSHMANA WAS VERY HAPPY.

WE'LL SOON DEFEAT RAVANA AND RESCUE SITA.

IT WILL BE DIFFICULT. BUT WE'LL SUCCEED.

AT LANKA —

MY LORD, RAMA AND HIS MONKEYS ARE CROSSING THE SEA. THEY'LL SOON BE ON OUR SHORES.

LET BHASMALOCHANA FIGHT THEM BACK.

WITH ONE LOOK, HE'LL DESTROY ALL OF THEM.

WHEN RAMA AND HIS ARMY REACHED THE SHORES OF LANKA —

WHO IS THAT STRANGE WARRIOR RIDING TOWARDS US? WHY HAS HE COVERED HIS EYES?

IT'S BHASMALOCHANA!

WHY DO YOU LOOK SCARED, VIBHISHANA?

WHOEVER BHASMALOCHANA LOOKS AT, IS REDUCED TO ASHES. HE'LL UNCOVER HIS EYES WHEN HE COMES NEAR US.

SHOOT HIM WITH MIRRORS! HE'LL SEE HIMSELF AND GET BURNT INSTEAD.

RAMA QUICKLY CREATED MILLIONS OF MIRRORS AND AIMED THEM AT BHASMA-LOCHANA.

BEFORE BHASMALOCHANA COULD UNCOVER HIS EYES, THE MIRRORS HAD SURROUNDED HIM.

WHEN THE TERRIBLE RAKSHASA OPENED HIS EYES, HE FELT HUNDREDS OF EYES BURNING INTO HIM. THEY WERE THE REFLECTIONS OF HIS OWN FIERY EYES!

NO!

AND THE NEXT MOMENT, BHASMALOCHANA WAS BURNT TO ASHES.

WICKED BHASMALOCHANA IS DEAD! VICTORY TO RAMA!

AFTER THAT, MANY RAKSHASAS CAME TO FIGHT RAMA. BUT ALL OF THEM WERE KILLED BY HIM. AT LAST RAVANA HIMSELF CAME.

RAVANA, GET READY TO DIE. NO ONE CAN SAVE YOU!

RIDING ON THE SHOULDERS OF HANUMAN, THE MIGHTY MONKEY-WARRIOR, RAMA LET FLY HIS ARROWS.

RAVANA TOO TOOK AIM...

...AND SHOT AT RAMA.

BUT RAMA WAS TOO QUICK FOR HIM.

STRUCK BY HIS DEADLY WEAPONS, RAVANA FELL UNCONSCIOUS.

AFTER A WHILE, HOWEVER, HE WAS ON HIS FEET AGAIN. BUT—

TAKE CARE OF YOUR CROWNS, RAVANA.

THE NEXT MOMENT RAMA FLUNG A CRESCENT-SHAPED WEAPON AT HIM.

AS RAVANA'S CROWNS FLEW FROM HIS HEADS, HE FLED.

TAKE ME TO MY PALACE. HURRY!

WHAT SHOULD I DO? WHEN I, THE KING, HAVE TO FLEE, WHAT HOPE IS THERE FOR MY SUBJECTS?

KUMBHAKARNA! WHY DIDN'T I THINK OF HIM? TO PICK RAMA UP AND FLING HIM INTO THE OCEAN WOULD BE CHILD'S PLAY FOR MY BROTHER.

GO WAKE KUMBHAKARNA UP! ASK HIM TO SEE ME.

IN HIS EXCITEMENT, RAVANA HAD FORGOTTEN BRAHMA'S WARNING. IF KUMBHAKARNA WERE WOKEN BEFORE THE SIX MONTHS WERE OVER, HIS LIFE WOULD BE IN DANGER!

THE RAKSHASA SERVANTS WENT TO KUMBHAKARNA'S PALACE.

KUMBHAKARNA WAS FAST ASLEEP. AS HE BREATHED OUT···

····THE RAKSHASAS WERE SWEPT OFF THEIR FEET···

···AND AS HE BREATHED IN, THEY WERE PULLED TOWARDS HIS NOSTRILS.

HELP!

I CAN'T SEE ANYTHING! WHERE AM I?

WE ARE IN KUMBHAKARNA'S NOSE!

THEN AS KUMBHAKARNA BREATHED OUT—

WE ARE OUT! SAFE!

HEY! HE'S BREATHING IN! HOLD ON!

LET'S GET BEHIND HIS HEAD.

HOW DO WE WAKE HIM UP?

LET'S MAKE A NOISE.

IT'S USELESS. HE HASN'T EVEN STOPPED SNORING!

THEY POURED ICE-COLD SANDALWOOD PASTE ON HIM.

HE'S ONLY SNORING LOUDER!

THEY BLEW CONCH-SHELLS NEAR HIS EAR.

BUT KUMBHAKARNA SLEPT ON.

THE RAKSHASAS WENT BACK TO RAVANA.

ALL OUR EFFORTS HAVE FAILED. KUMBHAKARNA IS STILL ASLEEP.

TRY BEATING HIM.

THE RAKSHASAS WENT BACK TO KUMBHAKARNA, WITH HUGE LOGS AND ROCKS...

...WHICH THEY FLUNG AT THE SLEEPING RAKSHASA.

THEN THEY BROUGHT ELEPHANTS AND MADE THEM WALK ON HIM.

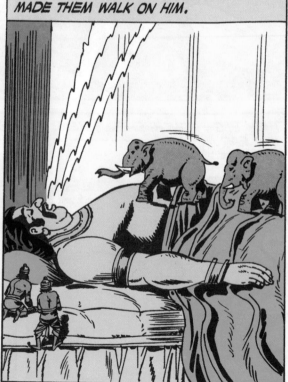

HOURS LATER—

THE ELEPHANTS ARE TIRED. THEY NEED REST.

TAKE THEM AWAY! LET'S DRAG HIM OUT OF BED.

BUT THEY COULD NOT EVEN MOVE HIM.

WE'LL HAVE TO THINK OF SOMETHING ELSE.

I GIVE UP!

I'M TIRED AND HUNGRY.

HUNGRY!

I KNOW HOW TO WAKE UP THE MIGHTY KUMBHAKARNA!

HOW?

BRING SOME STEAMING HOT FOOD.

WHEN THE FOOD WAS BROUGHT—

UNCOVER THE DISHES.

THE NEXT MOMENT—

HO! HUM! YAWN

WHO DARES DISTURB MY SLUMBER?

THE LORD OF LANKA WISHES TO SEE YOU.

I'M HUNGRY. I MUST WASH AND EAT, FIRST.

THE RAKSHASAS QUICKLY SET HUGE PILES OF FOOD BEFORE HIM.

MM—M—M! DELICIOUS!

AND NOW SOMETHING TO WASH DOWN THE FOOD.

WHY WAS I WOKEN UP? HAS INDRA ATTACKED US AGAIN? THIS TIME I'LL KILL HIM!

IT'S NOT INDRA BUT MEN AND MONKEYS WHO ARE ABOUT TO ATTACK LANKA.

KUMBHAKARNA LEFT FOR RAVANA'S PALACE.

WHAT CAN I DO FOR YOU?

WHO ARE YOU AFRAID OF? WHY THIS BATTLE WITH MEN AND MONKEYS?

IT'S A LONG STORY...

RAVANA TOLD KUMBHAKARNA ALL ABOUT HIS WAR WITH RAMA.

RAMA SEEMS TO BE A GREAT MAN. WHAT IF HE'S LORD VISHNU IN HUMAN FORM?

IMPOSSIBLE! HE'S ONLY A CUNNING MAN. HE MUST BE KILLED.

IT SHALL BE DONE. I'LL KILL OUR ENEMIES AND PROTECT OUR CITY.

I'VE NO DOUBT ABOUT IT. YOU ARE MIGHTY AND FEARLESS. I'M SURE YOU'LL SUCCEED.

KUMBHAKARNA MARCHED ALONE.

HE WAS FOLLOWED AT A DISTANCE BY TWO THOUSAND SLAVES CARRYING A HEAVY IRON ROD, THE WEAPON OF THE MIGHTY RAKSHASA.

THE EARTH SHOOK UNDER HIM...

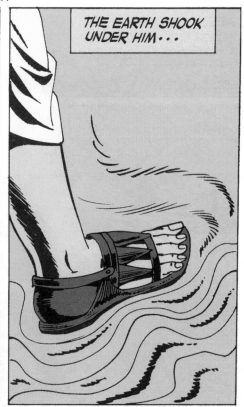

...AND THE WAVES ROSE HIGH IN THE OCEAN.

THE MONKEY-WARRIORS TREMBLED WITH FEAR.

WE'RE NO MATCH FOR THIS GIANT.

NEELA, A MIGHTY MONKEY, UPROOTED A HUGE SAL TREE...

... RAN TOWARDS KUMBHAKARNA...

... AND HURLED IT AT HIM.

BUT IT WAS THE TREE THAT BROKE INTO BITS!

RUN!

ARE YOU RUNNING TO FETCH MORE TREES? HA! HA!

SUGREEVA, THE MONKEY-KING, CHALLENGED KUMBHAKARNA TO A FIGHT.

HEY! KUMBHAKARNA, WHY DON'T YOU FIGHT WITH ME? I'LL KILL YOU WITH ONE BLOW.

KUMBHAKARNA HELD OUT HIS HAND FOR THE MIGHTY IRON ROD.

BUT SUGREEVA SPRANG UP...

... TORE AWAY THE ROD ...

...AND DASHED IT TO THE GROUND.

THE NEXT MOMENT KUMBHAKARNA PICKED HIM UP...

...AND MARCHED OFF TOWARDS RAVANA'S PALACE.

I'LL MAKE A GIFT OF YOU TO RAVANA.

ALAS! WE'LL NEVER SEE HIM AGAIN.

AS KUMBHAKARNA WALKED THROUGH THE CITY, THE RAKSHASAS MADE FUN OF SUGREEVA.

LOOK! LOOK! THERE GOES THE KING OF THE MONKEYS!

I MUST SAVE MYSELF SOMEHOW!

SUDDENLY, SUGREEVA TORE OFF KUMBHAKARNA'S EAR.

KUMBHAKARNA SHRIEKED AND FLUNG HIM AWAY.

SUGREEVA JOYFULLY BOUNDED BACK TO HIS ARMY.

KUMBHAKARNA WAS FILLED WITH SHAME.

THE GREAT KUMBHAKARNA OVERPOWERED BY A MERE MONKEY! OH, THE SHAME OF IT!

I SHALL GO BACK AND DEVOUR EVERY MONKEY ON THE BATTLEFIELD.

LOOK, WHO'S HERE!

HE STILL HASN'T LEARNT HIS LESSON.

CALL RAMA, OF WHOM I'VE HEARD SO MUCH. LET ME SEE HIM FIGHT.

28

HERE I AM. USE ALL YOUR STRENGTH. AFTER I'VE KILLED YOU AND RAVANA, I'LL MAKE VIBHISHANA KING OF LANKA, TAKE SITA, AND RETURN WITH HER TO AYODHYA.

YOU WILL NEVER SEE YOUR WIFE AGAIN. NOR WILL YOU RETURN TO YOUR LAND.

RAMA SHOT A DART AT HIM. BUT—

HA! HA! THAT TICKLES. NOW SEE WHAT I CAN DO!

AND KUMBHAKARNA RUSHED TOWARDS RAMA.

RAMA FIXED A SPECIAL ARROW TO HIS BOW.

THE ARROW FOUND ITS MARK.

AAGHH!!

AND KUMBHAKARNA FELL DEAD.

WHEN THE NEWS REACHED RAVANA—

ALAS! WHY DID I WAKE UP MY BROTHER IN SPITE OF THE WARNING?

I WILL AVENGE HIS DEATH. I'LL SLAY RAMA.

BUT IN THE BATTLE WITH RAMA, IT WAS RAVANA WHO WAS SLAIN. RAMA MADE VIBHISHANA THE LORD OF LANKA...

...AND RETURNED TO AYODHYA, HIS CAPITAL, WITH SITA AND LAKSHMANA.

AMAR CHITRA KATHA

ANNUAL SUBSCRIPTION FORM

GET THREE BESTSELLING AMAR CHITRA KATHA TITLES DELIVERED HOME EACH MONTH. START YOUR SUBSCRIPTION TODAY!

ANNUAL SUBSCRIPTION
MRP ₹2520
OFFER PRICE ₹1799

YOUR DETAILS*

Name: _____ Date of birth: ☐☐ ☐☐ ☐☐☐☐

Address: _____

City: _____ State: _____ Pincode: ☐☐☐☐☐☐

School: _____ Email: _____

Phone/ Mobile No.: ☐☐☐☐☐☐☐☐☐☐☐☐

PAYMENT OPTIONS

Cheque/DD: ☐☐☐☐☐☐ drawn in favour of '**ACK MEDIA DIRECT LTD.**' on bank _____

_____ for amount _____

_____ Dated: ☐☐ ☐☐ ☐☐☐☐ and send it to: AFL House,

7th Floor, Lok Bharti Complex, Marol Maroshi Road, Marol, Andheri East, Mumbai- 400059

*T & C apply

You can subscribe online at www.amarchitrakatha.com

*Please fill all the fields to activate your subscription. Please allow 4 to 6 weeks for the Subscription to commence.

For any queries or further information: **Email:** customerservice@ack-media.com | **Call:** 022-49188881/2

GHATOTKACHA

THE CHIVALROUS DEMON

The route to your roots

GHATOTKACHA

He may have looked like a demon, but Ghatatkacha was a guardian angel - always ready to help, always cheerful. The Pandava brother, Bheema, was lucky to have him as a son, for he saved his life more than once. And if it were not for this brave young rakshasa, the Kauravas may well have been the victors of the famous battle of Mahabharata.

Script	Illustrations	Editor
Lakshmi Seshadri	Umesh Burande	Anant Pai

Cover illustration by: Khalap

GHATOTKACHA

THE KAURAVA PRINCES AND THE ORPHANED
PANDAVA PRINCES WERE COUSINS. THEY GREW
UP TOGETHER AT HASTINAPURA IN THE
CHARGE OF THEIR GRAND-UNCLE, BHEESHMA.

BUT THE KAURAVAS WERE JEALOUS OF THEIR COUSINS.

UNCLE BHEESHMA IS PARTIAL TO THE PANDAVAS.

THE PEOPLE TOO LOVE THEM MORE THAN US.

JEALOUSY SOON TURNED INTO HATRED. DURYODHANA, THE ELDEST KAURAVA THOUGHT OF A WICKED PLAN.

WE WILL SEND THEM TO VARANAVATA TO LIVE IN THE HOUSE OF LAC. AND THEN SET FIRE TO IT.

WHEN THE PANDAVAS ARRIVED AT VARANAVATA, YUDHISHTHIRA, THE ELDEST OF THEM TURNED TO THE OTHERS—

THIS IS A TRAP!

THE PANDAVAS SECRETLY HAD A TUNNEL MADE FOR ESCAPE.

BEFORE WE LEAVE, WE MUST SET FIRE TO THIS HOUSE.

AFTER SETTING THE HOUSE ON FIRE, THE PANDAVAS AND THEIR MOTHER, KUNTI, ESCAPED THROUGH THE TUNNEL.

WHEN THEY WERE DEEP IN THE FOREST—

I AM TIRED, MOTHER.

I KNOW. BUT WE CANNOT STOP NOW. BHEEMA, CAN YOU CARRY HIM?

BHEEMA WAS THE STRONGEST OF THEM ALL.

I CAN CARRY ALL OF YOU.

WHEN THEY HAD TRAVELLED FAR ENOUGH—

NOW WE MAY REST.

YOU ARE ALL TIRED. I AM NOT. YOU SLEEP. I'LL KEEP WATCH.

HIDIMBA, A RAKSHASA WAS THE MASTER OF THAT FOREST.

SISTER HIDIMBAA! I SMELL HUMANS. BRING THEM HERE. WE SHALL FEAST ON FRESH MEAT.

M..M...M...M..! MY MOUTH WATERS!

WHEN HIDIMBAA CAME IN SEARCH OF THE PANDAVAS SHE SAW BHEEMA FIRST.

HOW HANDSOME HE IS! I DON'T WANT TO EAT HIM. I'LL MARRY HIM.

I SHALL CHANGE MYSELF INTO A BEAUTIFUL GIRL. THEN HE WILL FALL IN LOVE WITH ME.

MEANWHILE—

HIDIMBAA IS LATE. HAS SHE...? IS SHE...? NO IT CANNOT BE! YET I WONDER...

AS I SUSPECTED! SHE HAS CHANGED HER FORM AND IS MAKING EYES AT THAT HUMAN.

HIDIMBA CHALLENGED BHEEMA AND THEY FOUGHT.

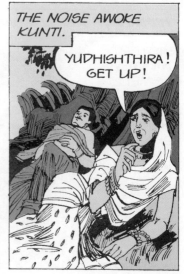

THE NOISE AWOKE KUNTI.

YUDHISHTHIRA! GET UP!

KUNTI, HIDIMBAA AND YUDHISHTHIRA RUSHED FORWARD.

BHEEMA! BE CAREFUL!

DO NOT FEAR MOTHER, YOUR BRAVE SON WILL WIN.

MY BLESSINGS, BHEEMA!

HIDIMBA WAS KILLED. KUNTI NOW TURNED TO HIDIMBAA.

YOU ARE VERY BEAUTIFUL! WHO ARE YOU?

THAT WAS MY BROTHER. I LOVE YOUR SON. I DESERTED MY BROTHER FOR HIM.

I HAVE NO ONE NOW. LET ME MARRY YOUR SON, MOTHER.

WE ARE HOMELESS.

I AM THE MISTRESS OF THIS FOREST. STAY HERE AS LONG AS YOU WISH.

KUNTI CONSULTED YUDHISHTHIRA.

LET HER MARRY BHEEMA.

IT IS ONLY FAIR, MOTHER.

SO BHEEMA MARRIED HIDIMBAA.

HIDIMBAA WAS A DEVOTED DAUGHTER-IN-LAW.

MOTHER, I MAY LIVE WITH YOU TILL YOUR GRANDSON IS BORN. THEN WE WILL HAVE TO PART.

NOT LONG AFTER, BHEEMA'S SON, GHATOTKACHA, WAS BORN. BEING A RAKSHASA HE KNEW ALL THEIR MAGIC AND WAS FULL-GROWN AT BIRTH.

FATHER! I AM THE LORD OF THIS FOREST. WHEN-EVER YOU THINK OF ME I WILL COME AND SERVE YOU.

WE WILL GO ON! GOD BLESS YOU.

THE PANDAVAS WENT THEIR WAY AND GHATOTKACHA LIVED WITH HIS MOTHER IN THEIR FOREST.

MANY YEARS PASSED BY. THE PANDAVAS BECAME THE RULERS OF INDRAPRASTHA WHERE THEY BUILT A BEAUTIFUL PALACE. YUDHISHTHIRA PERFORMED THE RAJASUYA SACRIFICE. THE KAURAVAS WERE JEALOUS OF THEIR SUCCESS.

WE MUST DO SOMETHING. THE PANDAVAS ARE TOO POPULAR AND PROSPEROUS.

I HAVE AN IDEA. LET US INVITE YUDHISHTHIRA TO PLAY DICE.

WE WILL MARK THE DICE AND CHEAT HIM.

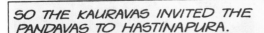

SO THE KAURAVAS INVITED THE PANDAVAS TO HASTINAPURA.

SHALL WE BEGIN?

A KING CANNOT REFUSE. WE WILL PLAY.

YUDHISHTHIRA PLAYED AND LOST ALL HIS WEALTH.

COME! STAKE YOUR KINGDOM NOW.

AGREED!

HE LOST HIS KINGDOM TOO. BUT HE CONTINUED TO PLAY.

WILL YOU AGREE TO GO TO THE FOREST FOR 13 YEARS IF YOU LOSE? IF YOU WIN I'LL GIVE BACK YOUR KINGDOM.

ALL RIGHT!

YUDHISHTHIRA LOST. THE PANDAVAS HAD TO LEAVE FOR THE FOREST, WITH DRAUPADI, THEIR QUEEN.

WHEN THEY HAD GONE, ARJUNA'S WIFE, SUBHADRA, A YADAVA PRINCESS, TOOK THEIR SON, ABHIMANYU, TO THE YADAVA KINGDOM.

ABHIMANYU, YOUR UNCLE BALARAMA HAS GONE BACK ON HIS WORD. HE IS GIVING VATSALA TO *LAKSHMANA.

MY REPUTATION IS AT STAKE. LET US GO TO DWARAKA.

ON THE WAY TO DWARAKA—

DRIVE QUICKLY, ABHIMANYU. I DON'T FEEL SAFE.

SUDDENLY—

HOW DARE YOU TRESPASS. I SHALL KILL YOU!

BUT ABHIMANYU WAS UNDAUNTED.

I'LL KILL YOU FIRST!

* DURYODHANA'S SON.

8

● BALARAMA'S DAUGHTER

AFTER A TOUGH FIGHT—

ALAS! HOW DID A MERE HUMAN OVERPOWER YOU?

WHO IS HE?

THE SON OF BHEEMA, THE PANDAVA.

I AM ARJUNA'S WIFE, SUBHADRA... MY SON...

STOP! ABHIMANYU! HE IS YOUR UNCLE BHEEMA'S SON! YOUR COUSIN!

BROTHER! FORGIVE ME! I DID NOT KNOW YOU.

SUBHADRA TOLD HER STORY.

SISTER! MY BROTHER, BALARAMA, HAS GONE BACK ON HIS WORD.

ABHIMANYU WAS BETROTHED TO HIS DAUGHTER, VATSALA.

BUT NOW THAT ARJUNA IS IN EXILE, VATSALA IS TO MARRY LAKSHMANA, THE SON OF THE KAURAVA, DURYODHANA.

WE ARE GOING TO DWARAKA TO TRY AND PREVENT IT.

GHATOTKACHA PROMISED TO HELP THEM.

DON'T WORRY, MOTHER! TAKE OUR GUESTS HOME. I WILL SETTLE THIS MATTER.

GHATOTKACHA CALLED HIS RAKSHASAS.

MEN! GO TO DWARAKA. BUY UP ALL THE SHOPS THERE AND...

WHEN HE HAD FINISHED—

THEN WAIT FOR MY SIGNAL.

THE RAKSHASAS WENT TO DWARAKA AND BOUGHT UP ALL THE SHOPS. THEN—

NEW CLOTHES FOR OLD.

DO YOU REALLY EXCHANGE THEM?

UNBELIEVABLE! SHOPS IN DWARAKA EXCHANGE OLD CLOTHES FOR NEW ONES.

THE KAURAVAS WHO HAD COME FOR THE WEDDING, FLOCKED TO THE SHOPS.

THESE NEW CLOTHES ARE OF A SUPERIOR QUALITY.

WHAT A NOVEL WAY OF ENTER-TAINING THE BRIDE-GROOM'S PARTY.

MEANWHILE GHATOTKACHA ENTERED VATSALA'S ROOM.

I COME FROM ABHIMANYU! READ THIS.

VATSALA READ ABHIMANYU'S MESSAGE.

COME! SIT DOWN AND DO NOT BE AFRAID.

MY LORD TELLS ME TO OBEY YOU.

GHATOTKACHA PICKED UP VATSALA'S BED AND FLEW OUT OF THE WINDOW.

YOU SHALL SOON BE WITH ABHIMANYU AND MOTHER SUBHADRA.

GHATOTKACHA LEFT VATSALA WITH ABHIMANYU AND RETURNED TO DWARAKA.

I MUST NOW TRANSFORM MYSELF TO LOOK LIKE VATSALA...

...AND TAKE HER PLACE.

THE NEXT MORNING THE BRIDE WAS LED TO THE MARRIAGE HALL.

I SHALL NOW SQUEEZE HIS HAND TILL IT BREAKS.

O..O..O! HOW TIGHT HER GRIP IS!

GHATOTKACHA SQUEEZED LAKSHMANA'S HAND SO HARD THAT HE FAINTED.

HA! HA!

AND GHATOTKACHA FLEW AWAY WITH HIS MEN.

COME! OUR WORK IS DONE. LET US GO!

WITH THEM THE NEW CLOTHES ALSO FLEW AWAY.

WE CAN'T EVEN GO AFTER THEM!

OUR CLOTHES ARE FLYING AWAY!

THE NEXT DAY, SUBHADRA ARRIVED AT DWARAKA WITH ABHIMANYU AND HIS BRIDE.

BROTHER! BLESS THEM! THEY WERE MARRIED YESTERDAY, THANKS TO GHATOTKACHA.

FATHER! FORGIVE ME! I LOVE ABHIMANYU.

I AM SORRY SISTER! I SHOULD HAVE KNOWN BETTER.

ABHIMANYU LIVED HAPPILY AT DWARAKA WITH VATSALA AND SUBHADRA.

WHEN THEIR EXILE WAS OVER, THE PANDAVAS RETURNED FROM THE FOREST. THE KAURAVAS WOULD NOT GIVE BACK THEIR KINGDOM. SO THE PANDAVAS COLLECTED THEIR ARMIES TO FIGHT THEM. LORD KRISHNA WAS ON THE SIDE OF THE PANDAVAS—

BHEEMA! YOU MUST CALL GHATOTKACHA. WE WILL NEED HIS HELP. DON'T YOU AGREE, KRISHNA?

YES. HE HELPED MY SISTER SUBHADRA WHEN SHE NEEDED HIM.

NOW HE WILL BE ONLY TOO GLAD TO HELP US.

I HAVE BUT TO THINK OF HIM.

GHATOTKACHA APPEARED WITH HIS RAKSHASA FORCES.

FATHER! HERE I AM!

THE MAHABHARATA WAR BEGAN. ON THE FOURTH DAY OF THE WAR, KING BHAGADATTA ATTACKED BHEEMA.

I WISH GHATOTKACHA WERE HERE TO HELP ME.

GHATOTKACHA AT ONCE CAME TO BHEEMA'S HELP.

THEY KILLED SO MANY KAURAVAS THAT DURYODHANA SOUNDED THE RETREAT.

WE HAVE DONE WELL TODAY, GHATOTKACHA.

17

THE NEXT DAY, BHAGADATTA RETALIATED BY ATTACKING THE PANDAVAS AND KILLING MANY OF THEM.

GHATOTKACHA CAME THERE. THE KAURAVAS SAW MANY OF THEIR FRIENDS LYING DEAD.

HOW DID SO MANY OF THEM DIE ALL OF A SUDDEN?

WH...WHAT... HOW? LET US SAVE OUR LIVES!

NOT REALISING THAT IT WAS MERELY AN ILLUSION, THEY RAN AWAY FROM THE BATTLEFIELD.

HA! HA! HOW EASILY THEY WERE TRICKED.

ON THE THIRTEENTH DAY OF THE WAR, ABHIMANYU WAS KILLED.

JAYADRATHA WAS THE CAUSE OF ABHIMANYU'S DEATH. ARJUNA SWORE TO KILL HIM BY SUNSET NEXT DAY.

IF I DON'T SUCCEED, I WILL KILL MYSELF!

DURYODHANA CALLED HIS GENERALS TO HIM.

WE MUST GUARD JAYADRATHA FROM ARJUNA.

IF HE IS ALIVE AT SUNSET, ARJUNA WILL KILL HIMSELF AND THE WAR WILL END.

BEFORE SUNSET THE NEXT DAY, ARJUNA, WITH LORD KRISHNA'S HELP, KILLED JAYADRATHA.

DURYODHANA TAUNTED HIS GENERALS, DRONA AND KARNA.

YOU HAVE NOT FOUGHT WELL. THAT IS WHY JAYADRATHA WAS KILLED.

DON'T BLAME US. WE DID OUR BEST.

WE WILL GO BACK AND CONTINUE THE BATTLE TILL JAYADRATHA IS AVENGED.

DRONA AND KARNA FOUGHT SO WELL THAT THE PANDAVAS WERE HARD-PRESSED. YUDHISHTHIRA CALLED ARJUNA AND KRISHNA.

MY ARMIES SUFFER! GO AND FIGHT KARNA.

IT IS NOT YET TIME FOR ARJUNA TO MEET KARNA!

LORD KRISHNA SENT FOR GHATOTKACHA. WHEN HE CAME—

DEAR GHATOTKACHA! HELP OUR ARMIES AGAINST KARNA.

I WILL FINISH HIM.

RAKSHASA-POWER INCREASES BY NIGHT.

I SHALL EASILY DEFEAT KARNA WITH MY MAGIC.

I WILL SOON BRING YOU HIS HEAD.

GHATOTKACHA MET KARNA AND ATTACKED HIM.

HE HURLED A SPARKLING *CHAKRAYUDHA AT HIM.

* DISC.

KARNA DESTROYED IT WITH ARROWS, SMILING ALL THE TIME.

GHATOTKACHA CREATED A MOUNTAIN BY HIS MAGIC. FROM THE MOUNTAIN CAME STREAMS OF WEAPONS.

KARNA DESTROYED THE MOUNTAIN WITH THE VAJRA ASTRA.*

* THE VAJRA ASTRA IS HARD LIKE A THUNDERBOLT AND CAN BREAK EVEN MOUNTAINS.

GHATOTKACHA MADE A DARK CLOUD WHICH RAINED DOWN STONES.

KARNA BLEW IT AWAY WITH A VAYU ASTRA.*

*VAYU ASTRA PRODUCES A STRONG WIND AS IT IS GUIDED BY THE GOD OF WIND.

GHATOTKACHA SENT TREES FLYING AT HIM.

KARNA DESTROYED THEM WITH ARROWS.

GHATOTKACHA FELL DOWN AS IF DEAD.

THE PANDAVA SOLDIERS GRIEVED.

ALAS! HE IS DEAD!

SUDDENLY THERE WERE GHATOTKACHAS EVERYWHERE.

KARNA SHOT ARROWS AT THEM ALL.

GHATOTKACHA OPENED HIS MOUTH WIDE AND SWALLOWED THE ARROWS.

KARNA ONLY SENT MORE.

GHATOTKACHA BECAME TINY AND ELUDED THEM.

THEN HE BECAME INVISIBLE AND SENT SHOWERS OF FIERY WEAPONS.

THE TERRIFIED KAURAVA FORCES APPEALED TO KARNA.

SAVE US, KARNA!

YOUR ARROWS ARE NOT POWERFUL ENOUGH.

YOU ARE OUR PROTECTOR.

USE YOUR SHAKTI!

THE SHAKTI HAD BEEN GIVEN TO KARNA BY INDRA, KING OF THE GODS.

IT IS MY WEAPON. IT WILL KILL ANYONE. BUT YOU CAN USE IT ONLY ONCE. IT WILL RETURN TO ME AFTER THAT.

KARNA HESITATED TO USE THE SHAKTI.

I RESERVED IT FOR ARJUNA! I MUST NOT WASTE IT.

BUT THE CRIES OF THE WARRIORS WERE PITIABLE.

WE CAN'T SEE THE ENEMY.

WE HAVE NO SAVIOUR!

YET THE WEAPONS HIT US.

I CAN'T LET OUR WARRIORS SUFFER.

I WILL HAVE TO USE THE SHAKTI.

KARNA PICKED UP THE SHAKTI AND THREW IT.

IT ENTERED GHATOTKACHA'S HEART AND WENT UP TO HEAVEN AS A FLASH OF LIGHT.

GHATOTKACHA KNEW HE WAS DYING. HE MADE HIS BODY ENORMOUS, JUMPED INTO THE AIR...

...AND FELL, CRUSHING A WHOLE KAURAVA REGIMENT UNDER HIM.

YUDHISHTHIRA TOOK GHATOTKACHA'S HEAD ON HIS LAP AND WEPT, WHILE KRISHNA LOOKED ON, SMILING.

ALAS! GHATOTKACHA, MY BRAVE CHILD! HOW CAN YOU SMILE, KRISHNA?

GHATOTKACHA HAS SAVED ARJUNA. KARNA'S SHAKTI IS SPENT. NOW HE IS POWERLESS TO KILL ARJUNA.

BHEEMA CAME TO MOURN HIS SON.

EVEN IN HIS DEATH GHATOTKACHA HAS HELPED US.

HE DIED IN A GOOD CAUSE. HIS DEATH WILL BE JUSTIFIED BY THE PANDAVA VICTORY.

Amar Chitra Katha's

EPICS & MYTHOLOGY

BRAVEHEARTS

VISIONARIES

FABLES & HUMOUR

INDIAN CLASSICS

CONTEMPORARY CLASSICS

EXCITING STORY CATEGORIES, ONE AMAZING DESTINATION.

From the episodes of Mahabharata to the wit of Birbal,
from the valour of Shivaji to the teachings of Tagore,
from the adventures of Pratapan to the tales of Ruskin Bond –
Amar Chitra Katha stories span across different genres to get you the best of literature.